Dear mouse friends, welcome to the

STONE AGE!

WELCOME TO THE STONE AGE . . . AND THE WORLD OF THE CAVEMICE!

CAPITAL: OLD MOUSE CITY

POPULATION: WE'RE NOT SURE. (MATH DOESN'T EXIST YET!) BUT BESIDES CAVEMICE, THERE ARE PLENTY OF DINOSAURS, <u>WAY</u> TOO MANY SABER-TOOTHED TIGERS, AND FEROCIOUS CAVE BEARS — BUT NO MOUSE HAS EVER HAD THE COURAGE TO COUNT THEM!

TYPICAL FOOD: PETRIFIED CHEESE SOUP

NATIONAL HOLIDAY: **GREAT ZAP DAY**, WHICH CELEBRATES THE DISCOVERY OF FIRE. RODENTS EXCHANGE GRILLED CHEESE SANDWICHES ON THIS HOLIDAY.

NATIONAL DRINK: MAMMOTH MILKSHAKES

CLIMATE: Unpredictable, WITH FREQUENT METEOR SHOWERS

cheese soup

milkshake

MONEY

SEASHELLS OF ALL SHAPES AND SIZES

MEASUREMENT

THE BASIC UNIT OF MEASUREMENT IS BASED ON THE LENGTH OF THE TAIL OF THE LEADER OF THE VILLAGE. A UNIT CAN BE DIVIDED INTO A HALF TAIL OR QUARTER TAIL. THE LEADER IS ALWAYS READY TO PRESENT HIS TAIL WHEN THERE IS A DISPUTE.

THE CAVEMICE

Geronimo

Trap

Thea

Benjamin

Bugsy Wugsy

Hercule Poirat

Grandma Ratrock

Geronimo Stilton

CAVEMICE

THE SMELLY SEARCH

Scholastic Inc.

Copyright © 2014 by Edizioni Piemme S.p.A., Palazzo Mondadori, Via Mondadori 1, 20090 Segrate, Italy. International Rights © Atlantyca S.p.A. English translation © 2017 by Atlantyca S.p.A.

The publisher does not have any control over and does not assume any responsibility for author or third-party websites or their content.

GERONIMO STILTON names, characters, and related indicia are copyright, trademark, and exclusive license of Atlantyca S.p.A. All rights reserved. The moral right of the author has been asserted. Based on an original idea by Elisabetta Dami. www.geronimostilton.com

Published by Scholastic Inc., *Publishers since 1920*, 557 Broadway, New York, NY 10012. SCHOLASTIC and associated logos are trademarks and/or registered trademarks of Scholastic Inc.

Stilton is the name of a famous English cheese. It is a registered trademark of the Stilton Cheese Makers' Association. For more information, go to www.stiltoncheese.com.

This book is a work of fiction. Names, characters, places, and incidents are either the product of the author's imagination or are used fictitiously, and any resemblance to actual persons, living or dead, business establishments, events, or locales is entirely coincidental.

ISBN 978-9-386-31319-5

Text by Geronimo Stilton
Original title *Per mille pietruzze . . . il gonfiosauro fa le puzze!*
Cover by Flavio Ferron
Illustrations by Giuseppe Facciotto (design) and Alessandro Costa (color)
Graphics by Chiara Cebraro with Paola Molteni

Special thanks to Shannon Penney
Translated by Lidia Morson Tramontozzi
Interior design by Becky James

First printing 2017
Reprinted by Scholastic India Pvt. Ltd.,
2017 (Twice)

Printed in India by Repro India Ltd.

FSC
www.fsc.org
MIX
Paper from
responsible sources
FSC® C047271

MANY AGES AGO, ON PREHISTORIC MOUSE ISLAND, THERE WAS A VILLAGE CALLED OLD MOUSE CITY. IT WAS INHABITED BY BRAVE *RODENT SAPIENS* KNOWN AS THE CAVEMICE.

DANGERS SURROUNDED THE MICE AT EVERY TURN: EARTHQUAKES, METEOR SHOWERS, FEROCIOUS DINOSAURS, AND FIERCE GANGS OF SABER-TOOTHED TIGERS. BUT THE BRAVE CAVEMICE FACED IT ALL WITH A SENSE OF HUMOR, AND WERE ALWAYS READY TO LEND A HAND TO OTHERS.

HOW DO I KNOW THIS? I DISCOVERED AN ANCIENT BOOK WRITTEN BY MY ANCESTOR, GERONIMO STILTONOOT! HE CARVED HIS STORIES INTO STONE TABLETS AND ILLUSTRATED THEM WITH HIS ETCHINGS.

I AM PROUD TO SHARE THESE STONE AGE STORIES WITH YOU. THE EXCITING ADVENTURES OF THE CAVEMICE WILL MAKE YOUR FUR STAND ON END, AND THE JOKES WILL TICKLE YOUR WHISKERS! HAPPY READING!

Geronimo Stilton

WARNING! DON'T IMITATE THE CAVEMICE. WE'RE NOT IN THE STONE AGE ANYMORE!

MYSTERIOUS MAIL!

It was a warm autumn morning and I was feeling mousetastic! There were no meteor showers, no erupting volcanoes, and no earthquakes. BONES AND STONES! It was a fabumouse cavemouse day!

After a light breakfast of fourteen Jurassic cheeses, ten Paleozoic cheese balls, and eight cups of frothy mammoth milkshake, I nimbly skipped to my office. (Well, more or less — BUUURP!)

Oh, I forgot to introduce myself! My name is Stiltonoot, GERONIMO STILTONOOT, and I'm the publisher of *The Stone Gazette*, the most famouse newspaper in the **STONE AGE** . . . probably because it's the only one!

I had just stuck my snout out of my cave, when I heard a flapping sound — **SWOOOOOSH!** — followed by a loud shriek:

"**MAIL!**"

Then . . .

Huh?!

BONK

A mail-a-dactyl dropped a stone slab on my head! Great rocky boulders — the slab was so heavy, it flattened me on the ground like a Jurassic cheddar pancake!

When I sat up again, I looked at the mysterious mega-slab and was shocked to see that it was from . . . SALLY ROCKMOUSEN. My archenemy Sally — the host of Gossip Radio, the rodent who spreads fake news all over Old Mouse City — actually wrote to me?! IMPAWSSIBLE!

Gossip Radio is *The Stone Gazette*'s biggest, most double-crossing competitor. Its headquarters are perched on top of a small hill. From there, Sally screeches the most inaccurate, dishonest, and just plain fake gossip in the Stone Age.

Sally's news is passed by word of mouth to other rodents and shriekers,

4

who then screech it to others. By the time the news gets to the last mouse, it usually **DOESN'T EVEN MAKE ANY SENSE**. Sally's stories get mouserifically **WARPED**!

What kind of reporting is that? Sally is a pawsitive fraud! I didn't even read her note.

As soon as I got to the office that morning, I was greeted by my assistant, WILEY UPSNOOT.

"Everything okay, boss?"

"See for yourself," I grumbled, handing him **SALLY'S** note.

He read the message carefully. "Boss, it's an **invitation**! Sally is inviting you to a mousestastic

Huh?!

???

team TREASURE HUNT!"

For all the thorns on a cactus!

"**What?! Are you sure, Wiley?**"
I asked.

Wiley handed the note back to me. "Hold
on to your cheese, boss — take a look!"

DEAR GERONIMO,

YOU ARE OFFICIALLY INVITED TO PARTICIPATE IN A
MEGA TEAM TREASURE HUNT ORGANIZED BY THE MOST
DISTINGUISHED REPORTER IN THE STONE AGE — ME,
SALLY ROCKMOUSEN! DO YOU ACCEPT? MARK THE
BOX OF YOUR CHOICE:

☐ I ACCEPT!   ☐ I CAN'T REFUSE!

☐ ABSOLUTELY!   ☐ SURE!

"NEVER!" I squeaked.

"Never say never, boss," replied Wiley.

"I refuse to go!" I said, shaking my snout.

He shrugged. "Whatever you say, boss, but did you see this?"

PETRIFIED CHEESE!

The back of the slab had another message chiseled in very, very, very small print:

IF YOU DON'T PARTICIPATE, GOSSIP RADIO WILL SQUEAK TO EVERY RODENT IN THE STONE AGE THAT YOU'RE AFRAID TO LOSE. OLD MOUSE CITY WILL FINALLY REALIZE THAT YOU'RE A TOTAL SCAREDY-MOUSE! SEE YOU TOMORROW MORNING IN SINGING ROCK SQUARE!

Crusty cheese chunks! How could Sally Rockmousen accuse me of such a thing?

Okay, so maybe I'm not the bravest mouse in the **STONE AGE**, but I've always worked hard, and I've never turned my back on a **CHALLENGE**.

"That really **toasts** my cheese!" I muttered. "I'll never go on Sally's treasure hunt — and I mean **NEVER**!"

SALLY ROCKMOUSEN

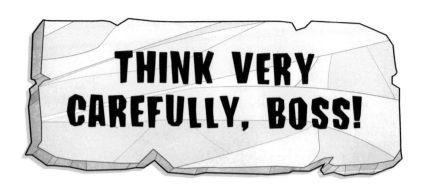

THINK VERY CAREFULLY, BOSS!

Wiley looked me square in the **EYE**. "I don't think that's such a good idea, boss."

"You're right, Wiley," I said firmly. "After all the dirty **TRICKS** Sally has pulled on us, I'm not going to fall for another one!"

"No!" he replied. "I mean that it's not a good idea to **refuse** Sally's invitation."

Rotten ricotta! Wiley was using the same tone of voice Grandma Ratrock used in the morning to get me out of bed for the gym.

"You definitely **HAVE TO** participate," Wiley squeaked.

"But . . . I don't **HAVE TO**!" I replied. "You see, I **HAVE TO** go to the dentist . . .

and I **HAVE TO** feed my autosaurus . . . and I **HAVE TO** work at the office, but —"

"That's exactly it!" Wiley squeaked. "The office! Work! The newspaper! If you don't participate in the TREASURE HUNT, how do you think that will make *The Stone Gazette* look?"

The truth was, WILEY was right. I couldn't refuse. I couldn't risk looking like an **unsportsmouselike** rodent. *The Stone Gazette*'s reputation was at stake!

"Oh, all right . . ." I caved.

Gulp!

We'll look bad!

I reluctantly began **CHISELING** a check mark on the invitation.

Once I finished, I scurried out of the office and started **LOOKING** for some other mice to join my team. And who do you think was the **FIRST** rodent to pop into my head?

You got it! The most famouse detective in the Stone Age: my friend **Hercule Poirat**!

THIS WHOLE THING STINKS!

I headed for Hercule's cave as fast as my paws would take me. But as I got closer, I didn't see the Paleozoic banana peel lying on the ground. I stepped on it, lost my balance, and . . .

WHoooooA!

I began slipping and sliding down the hill, faster and faster and faster!
Holey boulders, I was in trouble!

ZOOOOOOM

Oof!

I **rolled** along like an

avalanche

and crashed into Hercule's cave! Dazed, I stayed there **flattened** against the rock like a barnacle attached to a Paleozoic cliff.

UGH!

How prehistorically painful!

Hearing my **thundering** entrance, my friend Hercule scurried out of his cave.

"Pointy triceratops horns, Geronimo!

UGH

Couldn't you have just knocked?

Ouch!

Couldn't you have just knocked?"

I GR⊚ANED, massaging my bumps and bruises.

Once I got myself together, I told Hercule about the TREASURE HUNT.

"**Very strange!**" he remarked. "I'd better come with you. Who knows what kind of a mess you'll end up in otherwise!"

"It's settled, then — you'll be part of my **TEAM**!" I squeaked, relieved.

"Yes, but, Geronimo," Hercule said in a low voice, "this seems like a dirty trick. This whole treasure hunt thing STINKS even more than you do . . ."

I guess I hadn't bathed in almost a

MONTH — but how could he tell?!

"Let's see!" my friend pondered. "Our team is going to need someone who's brave, dynamic, and full of energy. In other words, we need your sister, Thea!"

"But she's not around," I answered with a frown. "She's on an expedition to the Land of Ice!"

THEA STEERING HER TEAM OF SLED-AUTOSAURUSES

"**Bones and stones!**" Hercule exclaimed, peeling a banana and looking disappointed. "Then who else are we going to recruit?"

"Well, we could ask Trap . . ." I suggested with a shrug.

"Fabumouse!" Hercule squeaked, cheering up. "At least we'll have a good supply of food!"

My cousin Trap runs the ROTTEN Tooth Tavern, which is famouse for its food. The chef, Greasella Stonyfur, makes whisker-licking good meals. YUM!

"We can ask my nephew Benjamin, too," I added.

"That's good," agreed Hercule, munching on another banana. "But we also need some female intuition!"

"Uh, female intuition?" I repeated, scratching my snout. "Who did you have in mind? **Harriet Heftymouse**, the village leader's daughter?"

"Of course not, Geronimo!" Hercule said. "We need someone who's more determined. Someone who's as **SHARP** as aged cheddar. Someone like your Grandma Ratrock!"

"But Grandma is at the **Great Gurgling Geyser** for her arthritis treatments," I explained.

Hercule **LOOKED** at me slyly. "Geronimo, no one else comes to mind? **No one?** I know someone perfect for our team — and for **you**!"

"W-wait a m-m-minute!" I stammered, turning as red as a Paleozoic **hot pepper**. "Y-you're not thinking of . . ."

"Of course I am!" Hercule said, grinning. "We'll ask *Clarissa Conjurat*, the shaman's daughter!"

"But . . . but . . . but . . ."

Hercule shook his snout. "No buts — I'm heading to her cave right now! In the

CLARISSA WITH HER PET DINOSAUR, FIFI

meantime, you go get Trap and Benjamin.
We'll all meet for dinner at the Rotten Tooth
Tavern!"

I stood there, as petrified as a block
of granite. You see, Clarissa is the most
beautiful, charming, determined, brave
mouse in the Stone Age. I have a huge
crush on her!

As it turned out, Clarissa accepted
Hercule's invitation without twitching a
whisker. But before she left, she stuffed her
purse with bottles and bottles of perfume
(lily of the valley, her favorite scent).

"You said that this treasure hunt stinks
of trickery," she explained with a grin, "so I
figured I'd better bring along a good supply
of perfume. It's going to be a smelly
search!"

SPRITZ! SPRITZ! SPRITZ!

As planned, we met that evening at the Rotten Tooth Tavern. Our team was now complete, and we'd named ourselves the Super Stiltonoots. We were ready for the most mousestastic TREASURE HUNT in the Stone Age!

Trap was jumping out of his **fur** with excitement. "This is going to be easy-cheesy! I'm a riddle-cracking genius!"

"**Actually** . . ." I started.

Trap grinned. "Do you remember the time I solved the brainteasers at the ICE AGE PUZZLES COMPETITION all by myself?"

I remembered that competition well — because I had whispered the answers to Trap! But this wasn't the time to **point** that out. Instead, I sniffed and noticed that *Clarissa* was spraying her lily of the valley perfume all over the ROTTEN TOOTH TAVERN.

"Fossilized feta!" grumbled

Greasella Stonyfur. Then she turned to Clarissa, frowning. "Are you trying to say that my restaurant **stinks**?" she asked.

"Of course not, Greasella!" Clarissa said with a **smile**. "Your tavern is squeaky clean. It's your customers who don't wash often!"

Greasella sniffed and made a

face. "FUNKY FUR! You're right!"

"I object!" exclaimed Trap. "I took a bath a month and a half ago!"

"And I washed myself about a month ago," I said. "I even lathered my WHISKERS!"

Greasella pinched her snout. "**News flash: You stink!**"

That's when we noticed that Hercule was unusually quiet. He looked awfully uncertain.

"What's wrong?" I asked.

"I was just thinking," he said. "I still feel like Sally's invitation is **very, very strange!**"

"I think so, too, Uncle Geronimo," BENJAMIN piped up.

"Yes," said Hercule. "Sally isn't the type to organize something without an ulterior motive, a trick, a SCAM, a —"

"Enough squeaking!" Clarissa interrupted him. "Let's have dinner and then get to bed. Tomorrow is going to be a long day, and it sounds like we need to be ready for anything!"

"I just had a thought!" Hercule squeaked. "Be sure to bring your **clubs**, and keep them close to you. With Sally, you never know what might happen . . ."

I was stunned.

Hercule was right!

Bones and stones!

I just had a thought!

What kind of the dangers would we face the next day? Thinking of the possibilities made my whiskers curl with fear. Squeak! But then a sweet voice said, "Good night, Geronimo!"

I turned to see Clarissa blow me a **kiss** and saunter off to her cave.

Ah, Clarissa . . . what a fabumouse rodent!

BY THE GREAT ZAP!

I suddenly realized something.

The treasure hunt might be dangerous, **TREACHEROUS**, and very risky — risky enough to make us extinct. But I would get to spend a lot of time with the rodent of my dreams!

GULP!

My whiskers quivered . . . but this time with *excitement*!

27

JURASSIC CHEDDARSNOUTS AND MEGALITHIC MICE

The next morning, we showed up at Singing Rock Square, as *fresh* and nimble as cricketosauruses. There were two other teams: the **Jurassic Cheddarsnouts**, led by Squeaks McStone, and the **Megalithic Mice**, led by Bobby Bouldermouse.

"Don't the Jurassic Cheddarsnouts look like a bunch of boneheads?" asked Hercule. "Beating them will be mouseling's play!"

I had to admit, the members of the first team did look like **boneheads**!

On the other paw, the Megalithic Mice looked like real **brains**! As I walked closer, Sally Rockmousen gave me a

dirty look. She stood between two enormouse rodents. **Squeak!**

"The rules are very simple," **Sally** explained. "You each have to solve a **RiDDLe** that will lead you someplace in the city. Once you get there, you'll find a second **RiDDLe** that will point you to the third **RiDDLe**, and then to the fourth, and so on until you find the TREASURE! The first one to the treasure wins. Simple!"

JURASSIC CHEDDARSNOUTS

Megalithic Mice

"Yeah, right!" Hercule whispered in my ear. "It may sound simple, but underneath it all, I smell a rat. Mark my squeaks!"

Sally handed out the first RiDDLeS to each of the three team leaders. Squeaks McStone, the Jurassic Cheddarsnouts' leader, was the first to read his note out loud:

"THe MOSt FaMOUSe raDiO SHOW iN tHe StONe AGe!"

"Hmm, could it be Gossip Radio?" asked Patty Rockington, one of the team members.

"It could be . . ." said her sister Tracy.

"Fabumouse! Let's go there now!" squeaked the third sister, Maisy.

Oh, for the love of cheese!

Gossip Radio was the **ONLY** radio show in the Stone Age!

Next up was **BOBBY BOULDERMOUSE**, who read the Megalithic Mice's riddle:

"GOSSIP QUEEN OF THE STONE AGE. HER NAME BEGINS WITH AN *S* AND ENDS WITH A *Y*!"

"It's Sally, of course!" Matt, Pat, and Nat Stoneford answered in unison. "Couldn't our riddle be something harder? Rats!"

"Don't COMPLAIN — now we know that we have to go to Sally's CAVE," replied Annie Ablepaws.

Now we know where to go!

Hercule had been listening to the other teams, too, and he **WiNKED** at me. "Pawsome! The riddles are all *easy-cheesy*! We've got victory in our paws, Geronimo!"

But maybe he had spoken **TOO** soon . . .

BENJAMIN THE BRAIN!

Trap, who had named himself our team leader, read our riddle and scratched his snout.

"Hmm. I don't get it!"

"Aren't you supposed to be the KING OF RIDDLES?" asked Clarissa.

"Sure as Swiss, but this is a Jurassic brainteaser!" Trap said. "Listen to this:

'WHEN HE'S FULL, HE'S LIGHTER!'"

We all twirled our whiskers and thought about it.

Fossilized feta! SMOKE was coming out

of our ears from all that thinking!

"The other two teams are already on their way," said Clarissa, "and we're standing here like **BOULDERS**!"

"Petrified Parmesan, it's not fair!" Hercule grumbled. "The other teams got **super-simple** riddles. I knew that rat Sally was going to trick us!"

"Let's not get discouraged," Benjamin squeaked. "Let's concentrate, instead. Who is lighter when he's full?"

"If you're full because you drank ten cups of steamy hot cheese, then you obviously don't feel lighter," Clarissa said.

"I agree," I put in. "And if your skin is full of megalithic mosquito bites, you definitely don't feel any lighter."

Crusty cheese crumbs! We weren't a single pawstep closer to solving the riddle!

All of a sudden, Benjamin remembered something. "I think I've got it! There's someone in Old Mouse City who becomes lighter when he's full — and then he FLIES!"

Clarissa jumped to her paws.

"Of course! Why didn't we think of it sooner? It must be a Balloonosaurus!"

We scurried toward Old Mouse City's
flightport as fast as our paws would
take us. That's where they keep all the
balloonosauruses that we cavemice use for
long air trips!

DID YOU HEAR ME?

The flightport was filled with balloonosauruses that were ready for takeoff. Some were filling up on flight fuel: **superbean concentrate** for the big ones, and SPICY SUPERBEAN

Screech!
Screech!

FLAP
FLAP
FLAP

CONCENTRATE for the faster ones. Gas from the beans is how they fly!

"Let's get our tails in gear!" I urged my teammates. "We have to find the tablet with the second RiDDLe!"

Easier squeaked than done! Where could it be? We SEARCHED everywhere. We looked between the balloonosauruses' paws: NOTHING!

We looked inside

Huh?!

the baskets tied to the balloonosauruses: NOTHING!

We looked along the balloonosaurus runway: NOTHING!

Then Hercule got a fabumouse idea! "Let's ask somebody for **HELP** — a rodent who knows the flightport well."

"Mouserific plan," Clarissa said. "How about the manager?"

Ah, *Clarissa* . . . what a determined mouse!

We found the manager easily enough. He was very, very **TALL** and very, very SKINNY. He was a rodent of few words — gruff but polite.

"If you haven't found what you're looking for among the balloonosauruses on the runway, try looking in their training pen," he suggested.

40

He led us to a FENCED-IN compound.

"This is where we train the baby balloonosauruses," he explained. "Here, they learn to stretch their wings and fly. They exercise until they're big enough to take flight on their own. And when they do, you can smell them coming from a thousand tails away!"

Blech!

CAN YOU FIND THE TABLET THAT HAS THE SECOND RIDDLE FOR THE SUPER STILTONOOT TEAM?

Answer:
Look in the superbean concentrate cauldron on the left page!

Slithering on our bellies, we approached the little **BaLLooNoSaURUSeS**. We didn't want to frighten them!

The compound was filled with cute but *lively* little balloonosaurus pups!

Trumpeting triceratops! They didn't stay still for a second! They skipped here and there, squealed and squeaked, and tooted away. (After all, they were full of superbean gas!)

PFFFFT! PFFFFT! PFFFFT!

"Maybe the manager is right," said Benjamin, covering his snout. "The RiDDLe could be inside the pen."

We wanted to look around, but the pups were so wild that crossing the PEN seemed impawssible!

But Clarissa took matters into her own paws.

"**STOP IT!**" she bellowed at the crazy pups. "If you don't stop moving around right now, I'll make you all take a bath — with soap! **DID YOU HEAR ME?**"

The pups froze in their tracks. Then, with their little tails between their **PAWS**, they trotted silently to one corner.

Ah, Clarissa — what a mouse!

Trap, Benjamin, and I searched all over

the pen, but Hercule was the one who finally found the tablet with the RiDDLe.

It was inside a big cauldron of superbean concentrate!

YUCK — this was one seriously smelly search!

The little tablet was chiseled with three words:

TaVerN
CaVerN
LaNterN

While Trap, Benjamin, Hercule, and I were deep in thought, Clarissa took the opportunity to douse us all with a triple dose of her lily of the valley perfume.

SPRITZZZZ!

Soaked in perfume, Trap cried, "Hey!

What in the name of all things cheesy are you doing?"

"OH, QUIT YOUR SQUEAKING!" she replied.

Clarissa sniffed us again and exclaimed, "Ugh! You **STILL** stink, even with all that perfume! You smell like rotten Jurassic jack cheese!"

Take that!

Groan!

ATTACK OF THE WIMPY JELLYFISH

Ignoring Clarissa's complaints, we read the riddle again. What did those words mean?

"**TAVERN** makes me think of the Rotten Tooth Tavern," Trap mused.

"**OF COURSE!**" exclaimed Hercule. "There's a **CAVERN** on the cliff next to the tavern!"

"And if there's a **LANTERN** inside that cavern, then we solved the puzzle!" Clarissa added.

Ah, *Clarissa* — what an intelligent mouse!

"So here's what the **RIDDLE** means: Get the **LANTERN** that's inside the **CAVERN** next to the **TAVERN**," Benjamin summed up.

We raced to the tavern, then borrowed a RAFT so we could paddle out to the cavern.

Trap was the **STRONGEST**, so he took the oars and began to row toward the cavern. But the current was strong, and our flimsy little raft began to rock BACK and FORTH and BACK and FORTH in the rapids. Petrified cheese — how

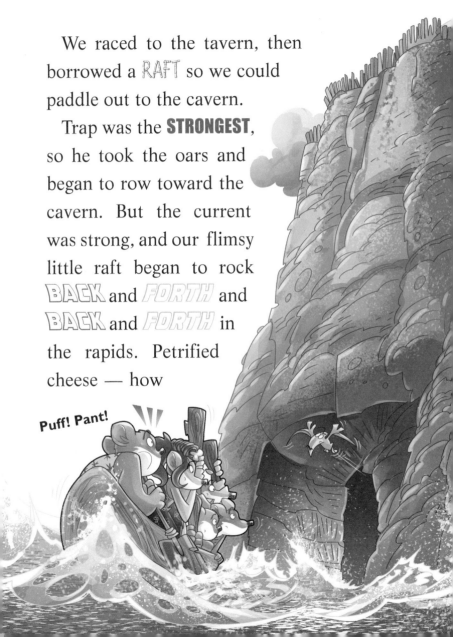

Puff! Pant!

prehistorically **SCARY**! We almost flipped over, and I was sure we were goners, but then . . .

"The lantern!" shouted Benjamin, pointing to the far end of the cave.

"I see it!" I cried, reaching out a paw. But as soon as I grabbed the lantern, I got hit by an enormouse

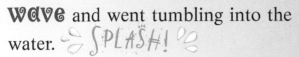 **wave** and went tumbling into the water. SPLASH!

Before I could twitch a whisker, a swarm of jellyfish stung me with their tentacles. **YOUCH!** What Paleolithic pain!

This was **not** going well.

"Don't be scared, Uncle Geronimo!" Benjamin said. "These are **wimpy jellyfish** — I recognize them. They only sting because they're frightened!"

SPLASH!

Help!

"That's right!" exclaimed Hercule. "They're not doing it on purpose — poor things!"

"Poor things?!" I squeaked as a jellyfish stung me under my tail.

"I know how we can get rid of those scared creatures without hurting them," Clarissa said suddenly. "The FIRE from the lantern will scare them away!"

Ah, Clarissa . . . she always comes up with such fabumouse ideas!

Too bad I was the one holding the lantern — so I had to SCARE the jellyfish away! I gulped, gathered my courage, and began to swing the lantern above the waves.

The jellyfish **fled** in fear. Holey cheese, it was a miracle!

Clarissa quickly extended an OAR and fished me out of the water. I was soaking wet, I was in **pain**, and I was clinging to the oar like an octopusaurus — but at least I still had all my fur!

COOL IT, GUYS!

I had made a megalithic fool of myself in front of Clarissa, but at least I had the LANTERN! Attached to the lantern, we found a little stone tablet that read:

FOR tHE NEXt riDDLE, GO
tO tHE MOSt CHARMiNG,
BRiLLiaNt, MOUSEriFic
REPOrtER iN tHE StONE
aGE: SaLLY ROCKMOUSEN!

My friends and I DASHED to Gossip Radio faster than saber-toothed tigers.

"**Ha, ha, ha!**" Sally cackled when she saw us. "Here comes the LAST team, led by the great riddlemaster, Trap Stiltonoot! **Hee, hee, hee!**"

Offended, Trap grumbled under his whiskers. "GRRRRRRRRRR..."

"Here's the lantern," said Hercule, trying to stay on task. "Now **fork over** the next riddle, Sally!"

"COOL IT, GUYS!" Sally said, flashing a shifty little smile. "Do you seriously still think you can **win**?"

Grrrrrrr...

"Why not?" asked *Clarissa*.

55

"Until the race is over, we're in it to win it!"
Sally snickered. "Keep in mind that the **Jurassic Cheddarsnouts** have already solved their third riddle, and the **Megalithic Mice** have solved their fourth!"

Benjamin and I exchanged a disappointed

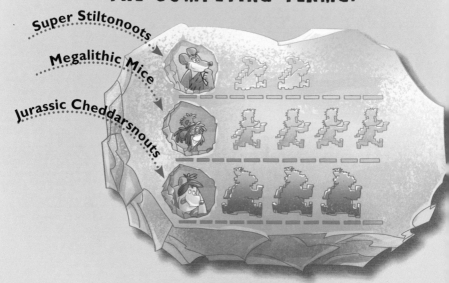

NUMBER OF RIDDLES SOLVED BY THE COMPETING TEAMS:

Super Stiltonoots

Megalithic Mice

Jurassic Cheddarsnouts

look. We were moving as slowly as a Stone Age snail!

"We can still do it!" Clarissa squeaked with determination. She turned to Sally. "What's the next RIDDLe?"

"Massive meteorites, if you insist — here it is!" Sally said, hurling the stone tablet at my snout.

BONK!

Rats! I rubbed my sore snout and tried to stay focused. Chiseled on the tablet was this riddle:

He Makes a saBer-tootHeD tiGer treMBLe.

"That's impawssible," snorted Trap.

"A saber-toothed tiger isn't **afraid** of anything!"

"You're wrong, Uncle Trap!" Benjamin said with a grin. "Saber-toothed tigers are afraid of **WATER**."

"**RIGHT!** I was just about to say that," Clarissa squeaked up. "But the riddle isn't about some*thing* — it's about some*one*! Read it again: '**He** makes a saber-toothed tiger tremble . . .'"

"Hmm." Benjamin **LOOKED** thoughtful. "If you were a saber-toothed tiger, who would you be **afraid of**?"

Let's see . . .

Trap tried to imagine he

was a SABER-TOOTHED TIGER. "Let's see. I'd have menacing eyes, big **TEETH** . . ."

"Big teeth!" exclaimed Hercule. "With such large **fangs**, those flea-infested felines must be worried about cavities!"

BONES AND STONES,

he was right! The thing that frightened saber-toothed tigers the most had to be . . .

"The dentist!" exclaimed Trap. "The answer is the DENTIST!"

"There's no time to lose," squeaked Clarissa. "Let's hurry to the Club Clinic, home of *Old Mouse City's* very best dentists and doctors!"

WHY, WHY, WHYYYY?!

While our team celebrated solving the riddle, Hercule pulled me aside.

"Geronimo, there's something about this whole treasure hunt that STINKS. Let's start sniffing around! Listen — *pssst . . . pssst . . . pssst . . .*"

My jaw dropped as I listened to Hercule's whispers. "Petrified cheese! WHAT are you squeaking about?"

I hung back to talk more with Hercule while Trap, Benjamin, and Clarissa scampered to the dentist to look for the next RIDDLE.

As soon as they **left**, Hercule said, "I

can tell that you're confused, so I'll try to explain the whole thing again." He looked me in the eye. "You know **why** we're dead last in the treasure hunt, right?"

"Uh, because the other teams are better than we are?" I guessed.

"**WRONG**, Geronimo!" he squeaked. "We're last because Sally gave the **easy-cheesy** riddles to the other teams and the **HARD-AS-BOULDERS** ones to us!"

At that moment, we saw the **Jurassic Cheddarsnouts** darting toward us, led by Squeaks McStone.

"Yoo-hoo, Squeaks!" Hercule called to him. "Would you please read us your **RiDDLe**?"

Squeaks showed us the tablet. It said:

WHat's tHe sQuare iN OLD MouSe City?

Pretty tough, huh?

?!

"Pretty tough, huh?" said Squeaks. "But Marty Mozzarella, the brains of our team, thought about it for a looooong time and finally figured out the answer!"

"Trumpeting triceratops!" I whispered to Hercule. "Any cheesebrain knows that it's Singing Rock Square!"

"Exactly!" Hercule said with a nod. "Did you notice anything else?"

I thought for a moment. "You mean that Squeaks STINKS like Jurassic jack cheese left out in the sun?"

"WRONG AGAIN!" Hercule grimaced. "Massive meteorites, Geronimo, try using that head of yours!"

"Hmmm . . . er, maybe . . ."

"Do I have to explain everything?" he grumbled, throwing his paws in the air. "Not only did we get the most **difficult** riddles, but we've also had to run from one end of the city to the other, covering tails upon tails upon tails."*

I scratched my snout. HOLEY CHEESE, he was right! "Huh, I hadn't thought of that . . ."

"Wake up, Geronimo! Sally is making us RUN all over the place, which keeps us far away from our caves!" Hercule concluded. "But why?"

Suddenly, I had an idea about what that rat Sally was up to. But . . . Noooo! It couldn't be!

STONE AGE NOTE:

*The basic unit of measurement in the Stone Age is based on the length of the tail of the village leader, Ernest Heftymouse.

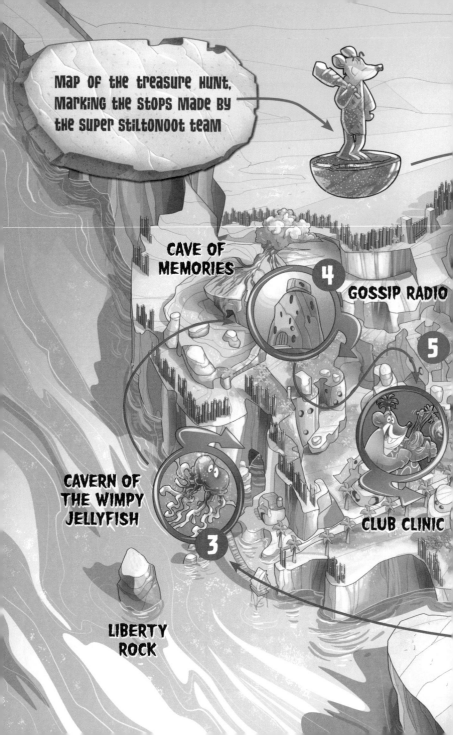

ARE YOU SURE YOU'RE SURE?

Cheese niblets! **Why** hadn't I realized it before?

Sally wanted to steal my **STONE AGE** scoop — a scoop so big that I was keeping it a secret. So secret that I had completely forgotten about it! That had been Sally's plan all along!

FOSSILIZED FETA!

"The **interview**!" I exclaimed. "The interview with maestro Samuel Songsnout!"

Hercule looked puzzled.

"**SAMUEL SONGSNOUT** is the most famouse musician in *Old Mouse City*," I reminded him. "In fact, he's the most famouse musician in the Stone Age!"

Hercule shrugged. "So what?"

"He's famous for two reasons," I said. "First, he invented the **Clubiphone**, a prehistoric instrument that is played by whacking clubs against horns, and second, he **HATES** doing interviews. Songsnout has never — and I mean **NEVER** — agreed to a single **interview**!"

"Aha!" squeaked Hercule. "But, Geronimo, you're not saying that . . ."

"As sure as squeaking!" I exclaimed. "Three days ago, I finally convinced him to see me. I snagged the very first and only interview with SAMUEL SONGSNOUT!"

"Did ANYBODY else know about the interview?" Hercule asked.

I shook my head. "Not a single rodent. I hid the interview transcript in a SECRET place only I know about!"

"Where did you hide it?" Hercule looked worried. "You don't have it with you now, do you, cheesebrain?"

"Don't get your tail in a twist!" I said. "I left it in my cave, in a very safe place."

Hercule tugged on his whiskers. "Are you absolutely sure? ONe HUNDReD PeRCeNt SURe? What if Sally found out about it from her shifty henchmice?"

I hadn't thought of that.

"Um . . ."

"And what if Sally organized this treasure hunt to keep you away from your cave and steal your interview transcript?"

"Um . . ."

"And what if we go to your cave and check things out right now?"

"Um . . ."

I turned as pale as a ball of mozzarella. Hercule was right! The *interview* transcript was no longer safe! What if Sally had gotten her PAWS on it? That would be unsqueakable!

"We'd better check," I said. We DASHED to my cave as fast as our paws could take us. When we got there, we peeked through the window and — holey rolling boulders!

"Sally's henchmice are in there!" I squeaked, tying my tail in knots.

GULP!

Two mean-looking rodents had snuck into my cave and were rummaging through **everything I owned**! What a prehistoric disaster! We had to think of a way to stop them right away!

A MOUSESTASTIC IDEA!

Luckily, Hercule was quick on his paws. **FAST** as a falling meteorite, he dashed away from my cave and waved for me to follow him.

"**Watch this**, Geronimo!" he said with a chuckle. Then he took a deep breath and cried, "Emergency at Gossip Radio! There's been a break-in!" A second later,

Sally's henchmice darted out of my cave and hightailed it to Gossip Radio. Bones and stones, what a relief! Hercule and I scurried into my cave as soon as the coast was clear.

"Hurry!" my friend instructed. "When those stonesnouts figure out there's no EMERGENCY, they'll be back in the twitch of a whisker!"

I quickly checked to see if my interview was safe. I was shaking with nerves from the ends of my ears to the tip of my tail! But it was still in its hiding place under my pillow, wrapped inside a palm leaf. Whew! The tablets were stacked like a book, and on the cover I'd written "SONGSNOUt INterview."

It's here!

"Prehistoric Parmesan! What are we going to do now? Sally's henchmice are going to be back any minute," squeaked Hercule, twisting his tail. "Come on, Geronimo. THINK!"

"Um, let's see . . ."

"Well? Come on. What's the plan?"

"Cave rats!" I said, annoyed. "Hercule, if you

keep interrupting, I'll hit you on the **snout** with my book of Greasella Stonyfur's most famouse recipes!"

Hearing that, Hercule looked at me with a **smile**. He picked up the book of recipes from the table.

"Of course! That's a mousestastic idea!"

Huh? What was he squeaking about now?

"These recipe **TABLETS** are the same size as the tablets you used to chisel the interview," Hercule went on. "Look!"

I examined the two books of tablets very closely. **Fossilized cheese crumbs!**

Hercule was right. The size and shape were **identical**!

75

"Listen carefully, Geronimo. We'll **swap** the covers! When Sally's henchmice come back, they'll take the wrong thing!" Hercule squeaked excitedly. "They'll grab Greasella's recipes instead of the **interview**!"

I had to admit, it was a **FABUMOUSE** idea. It just might save our fur!

Grinning, we switched the covers. Then we wrapped the recipe book (with "**SONGSNOUT INTERVIEW**" on its cover) in the palm leaves and left the actual interview (with the cookbook's cover) in plain sight on the table.

We left my cave feeling as proud as prehistoric peacocks.

"**Yoo-hoo**, Geronimo! Hercule!" someone called from the road. "We're here!"

It was Clarissa! She, Benjamin, and Trap were back from the dentist's office with a new RiDDLe in their paws.

It said:

> Paint your fur red —
> make no mistakes!
> Then scamper to where
> the latest news breaks.

AS RED AS FOSSILIZED HOT PEPPERS!

Wait one whisker-loving minute!

"Paint ourselves **RED**?" I cried. "Sticks and stones! That's impawssible!"

The **RED** ochre mine that is the source of all cavemice dye was thousands of tails away! It would take us a day to get there and back.

How many **seashells** would I have to paw over to get what we needed from the citizens of Old Mouse City to paint ourselves red? It ruffled my fur just thinking about it!

"I know what to do," Clarissa squeaked, before I could get my tail in too much of a twist.

We all LOOKED at her, intrigued. What could she have in mind?

"We'll paint ourselves RED with one of my new inventions!" she squeaked. "Come on, follow me!"

With that, we followed the fabumouse and brilliant mouse to her cave. There, she showed us her stone tub, where water from the Great Gurgling Geyser bubbled, super-pure and super-hot.

Where is it?

Clarissa went over to her

dresser and began rummaging through drawers of JARS, vials, and perfume bottles, until she finally said, "**FOUND IT!** Super-concentrated Jurassic beet juice!"

"What is that?" I asked. I had no clue what her plan was!

Clarissa opened the bottle, poured the contents into the tub, and . . . **BY THE GREAT ZAP**! The gurgling water instantly turned **BRIGHT RED** and fizzled with mousetastic bubbles!

"So . . . do we have to go in there?" I asked, worried.

Clarissa didn't bother answering. Instead, she gracefully jumped into the water. When she came out, she was bright red from head to tail. Ah, Clarissa — what an amazing mouse!

"Hooray!" exclaimed Hercule, Benjamin,

and Trap. Following Clarissa's example, they **dove** into the tub.

But I hesitated.

"Um, is the water very hot? What if the **COLOR** doesn't ever fade from our fur? What if my poor 🐾🐾🐾🐾 get boiled?"

Come on, Geronimo!

Um . . .

Woo-hoo!

Trap and Hercule finally dragged me into the tub, *kicking and squeaking*. When I climbed out of the water, I was as **red** as a hot lava pepper!

"What are we waiting for?" said Clarissa. "Let's hightail it out of here!"

Since the riddle said that we should "scamper to where the latest news breaks," we ran straight to Gossip Radio. When Sally **SPOTTED** us coming, she hastily hid something behind her back. Holey boulders — it looked exactly like the palm leaf–wrapped book that I'd left in my cave!

Sally's henchmice had fallen into our trap — they'd stolen the *recipes* instead of the real interview!

"What do you know?" Hercule whispered with a grin. "Our plan worked!"

Pretending we didn't notice the tablets,

we asked Sally for the next riddle.
   She handed us a tablet that read:

AS STRAIGHT AS ARROWS, THE SENTINELS CIRCLE AROUND. NOTHING BREAKS THEM, NOT EVEN A STONE FROM THE GROUND!

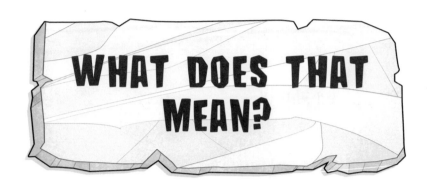

WHAT DOES THAT MEAN?

We were more determined than ever to figure this out and finish the treasure hunt. We got to work on the RiDDLe right away.

"Sentinels . . . hmmm," Clarissa said. "What do sentinels do?"

"They protect or keep WATCH over something," Benjamin responded.

Clarissa nodded. "Okay, so what could sentinels standing STRAIGHT as arrows be?"

"The riddle also says, 'NOTHiNG BreaKs them, Not even a stone From the GrOUND,'" Benjamin added. "What does that mean?"

"It means that the sentinels are strong!" I

said. "What if they're TREES?"

Just then Benjamin clapped his paws in excitement.

"No, they're not trees, Uncle Geronimo — they're POLES! The poles of the fence that goes around Old Mouse City!"

Hercule leaped to his paws. "Of course! They're **STRAIGHT**, they circle around the city, and they are **HARD AND STURDY** — so hard that not even a stone could break them!"

"Ugh, but there are so *many* of them,"

Let's see . . .

Trap said with a groan. "How are we supposed to find the next clue?"

Hercule knew just what to do.

"Simple. WE'LL SPLIT UP! Each of us will check a different section of the fence. Whoever finds the riddle first will alert the rest of the team with a whistle! Ready? LET'S GO!"

He handed each of us a wooden whistle and assigned us areas to investigate. "When you hear a whistle, drop everything and meet at Singing Rock Square."

We quickly rinsed the red dye from our fur — luckily, it was easy-cheesy to wash

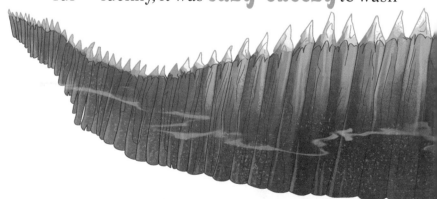

out! — and then took off to EXAMINE the fence. Benjamin and I worked together, while the others spread out around the city.

Benjamin was **scampering** from one pole to another when he tripped on a **ROCK** and fell. Petrified cheese!

"Are you okay?" I asked, crouching down by his side.

"Shhhh," he said, pressing his ear to the ground. He was listening attentively to something. BUT WHAT?

"Benjamin?" I asked again. "Are you all right?"

"I'm **fine**!" he said, his eyes wide. "But

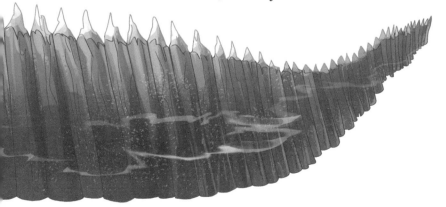

there's someone under here that isn't . . ."

What in the Stone Age was he squeaking about? I put my ear to the ground.

"HEEEELP!"

Bones and stones! Benjamin was right! Someone was **YELLING** for help underground. They could only be in **one** place — the

subwaysaurus tunnel!

I had to get everyone's tail in gear to help, so I pulled out my whistle.

TWEEEEEEEEEET!

A few minutes later, we all met at Singing Rock Square.

"We didn't find the next riddle, but we have to hurry!" Benjamin explained. "There's someone in DANGER in the subwaysaurus tunnel!"

"Fossilized cheddar chunks!" exclaimed Hercule. "Grab your CLUBS and let's get going!"

CHAAAARGE!

Together we raced **DOWN, DOWN, DOWN** under Old Mouse City into the metrocave, where the subwaysaurus lives.

"Try not to make any *noise*!" Hercule hissed at us. "You never know who may be —"

What happened?

Squeak!

"**HELP!**" someone yelled at the far end of the tunnel.

"**Someone rescue us!**" shouted a second voice.

"**SAVE US!**" screamed a third.

Slithering on our **BELLIES** like serpentsauruses, we finally came to the end of the **tunnel**. What we saw left me squeakless!

Shhh . . . quiet!

It was the **Jurassic Cheddarsnouts** and the **Megalithic Mice**! They were **TIED** up like balls of mozzarella . . . and they were surrounded by a gang of saber-toothed tigers. Fossilized feta!

Even worse, we saw **TIGER KHAN**,

the chief of the Saber-Toothed Squad and the most ferocious, evil FANGED feline in the entire STONE AGE!

I was shaking in my fur and preparing myself for premature extinction when Hercule came up with a mousestastic plan.

"I've got an idea!" he squeaked quietly. "They haven't spotted us yet, so we'll use the element of surprise. By sneaking through the tunnel's shadows, we can spook those overgrown cats and pretend we're prehistoric monsters!"

Even though I didn't want to get anywhere near those giant fanged felines, I had to admit — Hercule's plan could work!

We tiptoed quietly down the last few steps into an alcove. The Saber-Toothed Squad still couldn't SEE us, but we could see them. Once we had all reached the bottom,

Clarissa raised her club and squeaked bravely:

"CAVEMICE, CHAAAARGE!"

Side by side, we followed her, staying in the tunnel's shadows. We had to rescue our captured fellow cavemice!

AH, CLARISSA . . . WHAT A MOUSE!

Clarissa ran toward the saber-toothed tigers with a valiant cry. "**YAAAAAHHH!**"

Hercule, Trap, Benjamin, and I imitated her, vying to see who could squeak loudest.

"**YAAAAAHHH!**"
"**UUUUUGHH!**"
"**AAAAAAYAAAHHHH!**"

When the saber-toothed tigers saw the shadows of us with our clubs raised, they began to shake like Paleozoic pudding!

"**Monsters!**" cried **TIGER KHAN**, shaking in his fur.

Then they all turned tail as we swung our clubs and started *chasing* them away!

Then we heard thundering pawsteps coming down the tunnel. Holey cheese — all that **racket** had attracted the attention of rodents aboveground, who were RUNNING to help us!

Run for your life!

Help!

The village chief, Ernest Heftymouse, and his wife, Chattina, scurried **DOWN** the subwaysaurus tunnel, followed by a group of cavemice armed with **CLUBS**.

"Take that!" shrieked Chattina, swinging at Tiger Khan. "And that! And that!"

BONK! CLUNK! KAPOW!

Defeated and outnumbered, the Saber-Toothed Squad hightailed it away, slipping out through a **hole** in the tunnel.

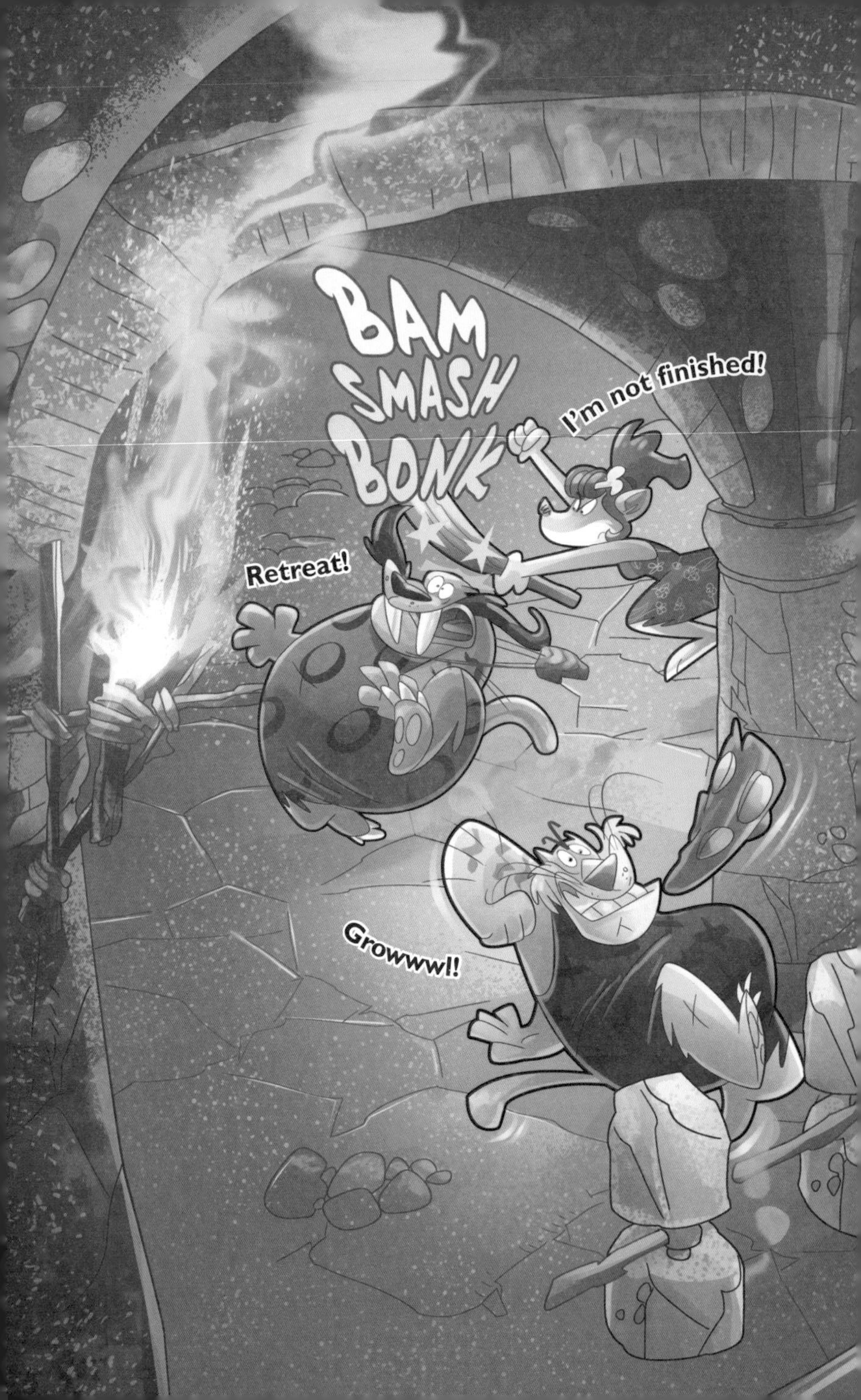
BAM
SMASH
BONK
I'm not finished!
Retreat!
Growwwl!

"You were lucky Benjamin heard you!" Hercule squeaked to the Jurassic Cheddarsnouts and Megalithic Mice as he untied them. "If we hadn't ARRIVED when we did, you would have been mouse meatballs!"

When we all got back aboveground, we were carried in TRIUMPH through the streets of Old Mouse City. Everyone cheered and clapped their paws.

"Hooray, Clarissa!"

"Hooray, Geronimo!"

"HOORAY, TRAP!"

"Hooray, Benjamin!"

For all the cheddar in the Stone Age! What a prehistoric moment!

JUSTICE IS SERVED!

The only thing left to do was to finish the TREASURE HUNT and find the hidden treasure! Easier squeaked than done . . .

"Our clues led us here, to this part of the **subwaysaurus** tunnel," said Squeaks McStone.

"Yes," Bobby Bouldermouse agreed, **pointing** to a dot on the ground nearby. "Ours do, too!"

The two teams began to **dig** as fast as their paws could go.

Scratch, scratch, scratch!

After some digging, they found a big

bag filled with **seashells**! What a Paleozoic prize! Since both teams had won, they divided the treasure equally.

When we got out of the subwaysaurus tunnel, Clarissa made Hercule, Trap, Benjamin, and me all take baths. Rats! The bath wasn't just to make us look more presentable — Clarissa mainly wanted to get rid of our Jurassic stench!

After we bathed, we headed to Gossip Radio for the official end to the TREASURE HUNT. As Sally announced the winners, she made sure to point out, "Geronimo, your team was dead last! HEE, HEE, HEE!"

Squeaks McStone spoke up. "Maybe, but Geronimo and his team saved Old

Mouse City from TIGER KHAN and the Saber-Toothed Squad!"

"Exactly," Bobby Bouldermouse agreed. "To **thank** him and his team, I think we should have a party in their honor!"

A cheer went up in the crowd.

"But before we do that," Hercule said, "there's something you all need to know. The TREASURE HUNT was actually an enormouse scam! Sally gave our team RiDDLeS that were harder than giant boulders. While we were distracted, she tried to steal an important interview that's supposed to be published in *The Stone Gazette*!"

Sally's eyes widened, and her mouth hung open.

"Fess up, Sally!" Hercule said, looking her **straight** in the eyes. "**YOU** stole

Geronimo's interview with Samuel Songsnout!"

Sally scowled. "**Whaaat?** No, I didn't! That article is mine, and I'll prove it! **LOOK!**" Sally held the tablets she'd taken from my cave, with "**SONGSNOUT INTERVIEW**" chiseled on the cover. "I have it right here. I'm the one who *squeaked out* an interview with the secretive Songsnout — not that **rotten-smelling** reporter rodent!"

"Fine!" said Hercule. "Then prove it. Why don't you read us a few lines of the interview, just to give us a sneak preview?"

Tell the truth!

Sally took off the cover of the **taBLet** and began to read. "Here it is: 'Greasella Stonyfur's Recipes: Special Dishes for the Discerning Rat.' Wait, **WHAT**?"

Sally stopped squeaking and turned as **red** as the lava from the Cheddar Volcano!

"Go ahead, Sally. Why don't you continue **reading**?" asked Hercule.

Sally shot her henchmice a dirty look. They tried to make themselves look very small.

Look at this!

SONGSNOUT INTERVIEW

"Uh, well . . . the lighting isn't very good here . . ." she mumbled.

As Sally tried to find an excuse, I scurried back to my cave and grabbed the **real** interview.

106

"Cavemice of Old Mouse City, look at this!" I called, returning to the crowd. "Sally is lying — this is the real interview! The one I'm holding in my own two paws!"

Sally finally exploded, SCREECHING at her henchmice, "You couldn't even steal the right tablets? YOU'RE FIRED!"

"I've heard enough!" Ernest Heftymouse thundered. "Sally, you lie more than a bed of rocks. I'm afraid I'll have to ban you from the celebration. Everyone else is invited to the Rotten Tooth Tavern at sunset!"

We all scurried away to our caves to get ready for the party. When we met again at the tavern, I sat next to the beautiful, moustastic, fabumouse Clarissa.

"Hi, Geronimo!" she squeaked.

I tugged on my whiskers. "H-h-hi, C-Clarissa . . ."

I was gearing up for a romantic speech that I'd practiced, but before I could say anything, Hercule attacked a bowl of **FOSSILIZED FONTINA DIP** with such gusto that it spilled all over me. **WHAT A MESS!**

"Geronimo!" Clarissa cried, wiping the cheese from her fur. "Maybe we can sit

together when you learn better **table** manners!" Before I could even squeak, she got to her paws and walked away. Sigh!

Aside from that tiny detail, the party was mouserific. We'd had quite an ADVENTURE! We may have lost the treasure hunt, but we saved Old Mouse City from the Saber-Toothed Squad. And for us cavemice, a fabumouse feast with friends is always the best reward!

I'll be on the lookout for my next adventure in the Stone Age, or I'm not . . .

Don't miss any adventures of the cavemice!

#1 The Stone of Fire

#2 Watch Your Tail!

#3 Help, I'm in Hot Lava!

#4 The Fast and the Frozen

#5 The Great Mouse Race

#6 Don't Wake the Dinosaur!

#7 I'm a Scaredy-Mouse!

#8 Surfing for Secrets

#9 Get the Scoop, Geronimo!

#10 My Autosaurus Will Win!

#11 Sea Monster Surprise

#12 Paws Off the Pearl!

#13 The Smelly Search

#14 Shoo, Caveflies!

Be sure to read all my fabumouse adventures!

#1 Lost Treasure of the Emerald Eye

#2 The Curse of the Cheese Pyramid

#3 Cat and Mouse in a Haunted House

#4 I'm Too Fond of My Fur!

#5 Four Mice Deep in the Jungle

#6 Paws Off, Cheddarface!

#7 Red Pizzas for a Blue Count

#8 Attack of the Bandit Cats

#9 A Fabumouse Vacation for Geronimo

#10 All Because of a Cup of Coffee

#11 It's Halloween, You 'Fraidy Mouse!

#12 Merry Christmas, Geronimo!

#13 The Phantom of the Subway

#14 The Temple of the Ruby of Fire

#15 The Mona Mousa Code

#16 A Cheese-Colored Camper

#17 Watch Your Whiskers, Stilton!

#18 Shipwreck on the Pirate Islands

#19 My Name Is Stilton, Geronimo Stilton

#20 Surf's Up, Geronimo!

#21 The Wild, Wild West

#22 The Secret of Cacklefur Castle

A Christmas Tale

#23 Valentine's Day
Disaster

#24 Field Trip to
Niagara Falls

#25 The Search for
Sunken Treasure

#26 The Mummy
with No Name

#27 The Christmas
Toy Factory

#28 Wedding
Crasher

#29 Down and Out
Down Under

#30 The Mouse Island
Marathon

#31 The Mysterious
Cheese Thief

Christmas Catastrophe

#32 Valley of the
Giant Skeletons

#33 Geronimo and the
Gold Medal Mystery

#34 Geronimo Stilton,
Secret Agent

#35 A Very Merry
Christmas

#36 Geronimo's
Valentine

#37 The Race Across
America

#38 A Fabumouse
School Adventure

#39 Singing Sensation

#40 The Karate Mouse

#41 Mighty Mount
Kilimanjaro

#42 The Peculiar
Pumpkin Thief

#43 I'm Not a
Supermouse!

#44 The Giant
Diamond Robbery

#45 Save the White
Whale!

#46 The Haunted
Castle

#47 Run for the Hills, Geronimo!

#48 The Mystery in Venice

#49 The Way of the Samurai

#50 This Hotel Is Haunted!

#51 The Enormouse Pearl Heist

#52 Mouse in Space!

#53 Rumble in the Jungle

#54 Get into Gear, Stilton!

#55 The Golden Statue Plot

#56 Flight of the Red Bandit

The Hunt for the Golden Book

#57 The Stinky Cheese Vacation

#58 The Super Chef Contest

#59 Welcome to Moldy Manor

The Hunt for the Curious Cheese

#60 The Treasure of Easter Island

#61 Mouse House Hunter

#62 Mouse Overboard!

The Hunt for the Secret Papyrus

#63 The Cheese Experiment

#64 Magical Mission

#65 Bollywood Burglary

The Hunt for the Hundredth Key

#66 Operation: Secret Recipe

Don't miss any of my special edition adventures!

THE KINGDOM OF FANTASY

THE QUEST FOR PARADISE:
THE RETURN TO THE KINGDOM OF FANTASY

THE AMAZING VOYAGE:
THE THIRD ADVENTURE IN THE KINGDOM OF FANTASY

THE DRAGON PROPHECY:
THE FOURTH ADVENTURE IN THE KINGDOM OF FANTASY

THE VOLCANO OF FIRE:
THE FIFTH ADVENTURE IN THE KINGDOM OF FANTASY

THE SEARCH FOR TREASURE:
THE SIXTH ADVENTURE IN THE KINGDOM OF FANTASY

THE ENCHANTED CHARMS:
THE SEVENTH ADVENTURE IN THE KINGDOM OF FANTASY

THE PHOENIX OF DESTINY:
AN EPIC KINGDOM OF FANTASY ADVENTURE

THE HOUR OF MAGIC:
THE EIGHTH ADVENTURE IN THE KINGDOM OF FANTASY

THE WIZARD'S WAND:
THE NINTH ADVENTURE IN THE KINGDOM OF FANTASY

THE SHIP OF SECRETS:
THE TENTH ADVENTURE IN THE KINGDOM OF FANTASY

THE JOURNEY THROUGH TIME

BACK IN TIME:
THE SECOND JOURNEY THROUGH TIME

THE RACE AGAINST TIME:
THE THIRD JOURNEY THROUGH TIME

LOST IN TIME:
THE FOURTH JOURNEY THROUGH TIME

Meet
CREEPELLA VON CACKLEFUR

I, *Geronimo Stilton*, have a lot of mouse friends, but none as **spooky** as my friend CREEPELLA VON CACKLEFUR! She is an enchanting and MYSTERIOUS mouse with a pet bat named **Bitewing**. YIKES! I'm a real 'fraidy mouse, but even I think CREEPELLA and her family are AWFULLY fascinating. I can't wait for you to read all about CREEPELLA in these a-mouse-ly funny and **spectacularly spooky** tales!

#1 The Thirteen Ghosts

#2 Meet Me in Horrorwood

#3 Ghost Pirate Treasure

#4 Return of the Vampire

#5 Fright Night

#6 Ride for Your Life!

#7 A Suitcase Full of Ghosts

#8 The Phantom of the Theater

#9 The Haunted Dinosaur

MEET
Geronimo Stiltonord

He is a mouseking — the Geronimo Stilton of the ancient far north! He lives with his brawny and brave clan in the village of Mouseborg. From sailing frozen waters to facing fiery dragons, every day is an adventure for the micekings!

#1 Attack of the Dragons

#2 The Famouse Fjord Race

#3 Pull the Dragon's Tooth!

#4 Stay Strong, Geronimo!

#5 The Mysterious Message

MEET GERONIMO STILTONIX

He is a spacemouse — the Geronimo Stilton of a parallel universe! He is captain of the spaceship *MouseStar 1*. While flying through the cosmos, he visits distant planets and meets crazy aliens. His adventures are out of this world!

#1 Alien Escape

#2 You're Mine, Captain!

#3 Ice Planet Adventure

#4 The Galactic Goal

#5 Rescue Rebellion

#6 The Underwater Planet

#7 Beware! Space Junk!

#8 Away in a Star Sled

#9 Slurp Monster Showdown

#10 Pirate Spacecat Attack

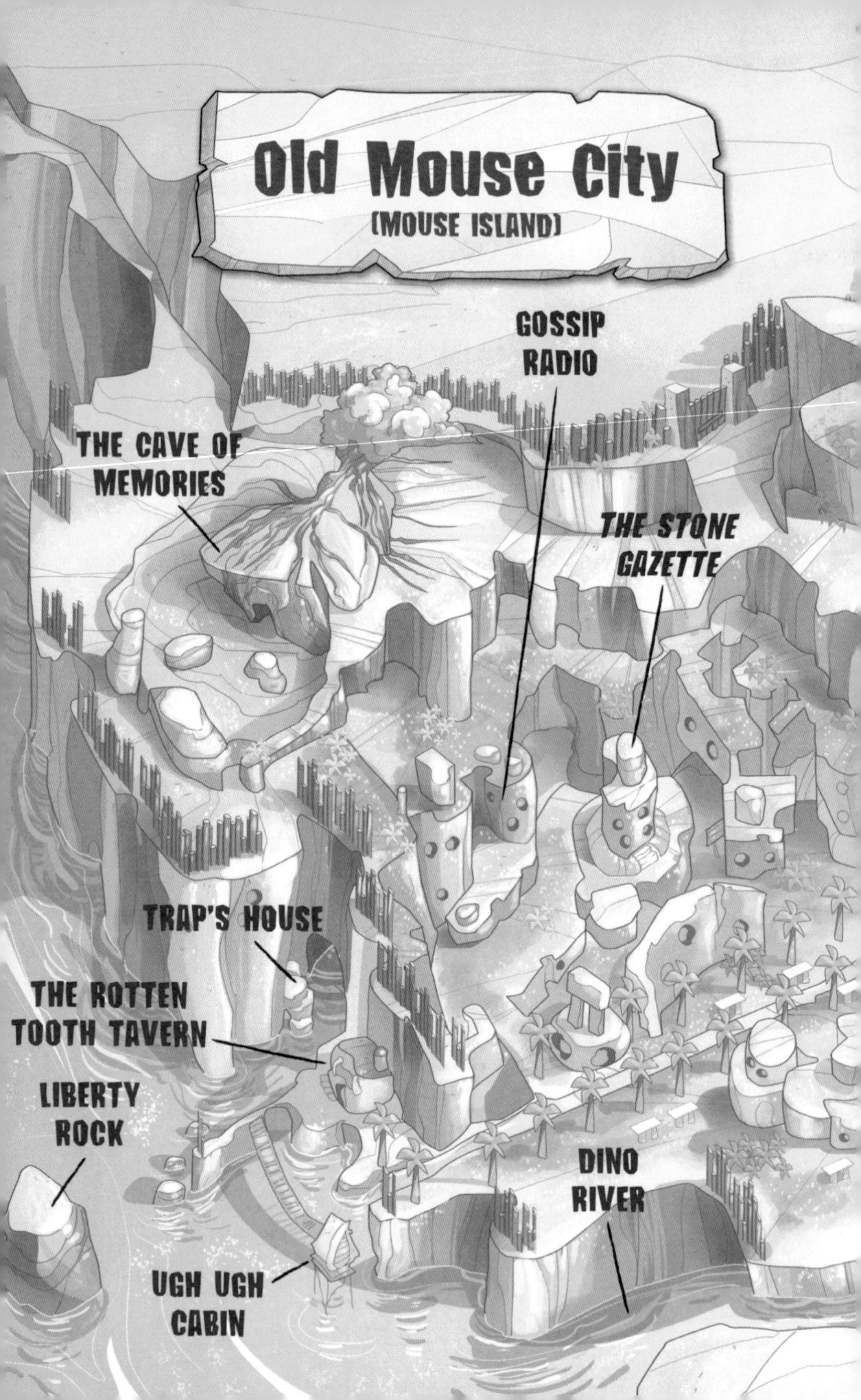

Old Mouse City

(MOUSE ISLAND)

GOSSIP RADIO

THE CAVE OF MEMORIES

THE STONE GAZETTE

TRAP'S HOUSE

THE ROTTEN TOOTH TAVERN

LIBERTY ROCK

DINO RIVER

UGH UGH CABIN

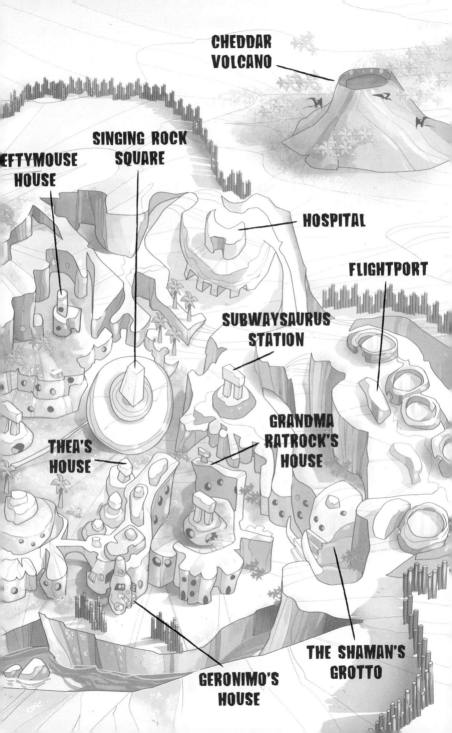

CHEDDAR VOLCANO

SINGING ROCK SQUARE

EFTYMOUSE HOUSE

HOSPITAL

FLIGHTPORT

SUBWAYSAURUS STATION

THEA'S HOUSE

GRANDMA RATROCK'S HOUSE

GERONIMO'S HOUSE

THE SHAMAN'S GROTTO

DEAR MOUSE FRIENDS,
THANKS FOR READING,
AND GOOD-BYE UNTIL
THE NEXT BOOK!